31901070202926

Roller Coaster

Adaptation by Monica Perez
Based on the TV series teleplay
written by Lazar Saric

CLARION BOOKS
An Imprint of HarperCollinsPublishers

Clarion Books is an imprint of HarperCollins Publishers.

I Can Read ® and I Can Read Book ® are trademarks of HarperCollins Publishers.
Curious George ® Roller Coaster
Adaptation by Monica Perez. Based on the TV series teleplay written by Lazar Saric.
Copyright © 2007 by Universal Studios
Curious George ® and related characters, created by Margret and H. A. Rey, are copyrighted and
trademarked by HarperCollins Publishers and used under license. Curious George ® television series
merchandise licensed by Universal Studios Licensing LLC. Published by special arrangement with
HarperCollins Publishers.

Library of Congress Control Number: 2023937405
ISBN 978-0-06-332351-3
ISBN 978-0-06-332350-6 (pbk.)

Book design by Rick Farley
23 24 25 26 27 LB 10 9 8 7 6 5 4 3 2 1
First Edition

George woke his friend up early.

Today was a special day.

They were going to Zany Island!

George was curious about riding
the roller coaster.
It was called the Turbo Python 3000.

It looked scary and fun.

Betsy and Steve had ridden it

nine times!

They invited George
to ride with them.
But there was a problem.
George was too short.

The man at the gate said

George needed to be

five candy strings tall to ride.

George was only four.

How could George grow

one candy string in a day?

Maybe he could eat leaves

like a giraffe. Giraffes were tall.

Yuck! The leaves tasted bad.

George took a bite

of his candy string.

Candy tasted better.

What else could he do to grow?

George thought exercising

might help.

He lifted a heavy bar.

Then George measured himself.

He was now four and a half

candy strings tall!

George wondered if stretching

would make him grow.

He tried it.

By this time George was very tired.

He nibbled on his candy some more.

George saw a mother and baby.

The mother told the baby

that sleep would help him grow.

So George took a nap too.

When he woke,

he measured again.

Hooray! He was finally

five candy strings tall.

But the sign said he was still
too short to ride.
How could that be?

"Have you been biting
your candy strings, George?"
the man with the yellow hat asked.
George nodded.

"When the candy strings were longer,

it took four to measure you,"

the man explained.

"Now that the candy strings

are shorter, it takes more of them

to measure you—five.

But you did not grow."

George was so disappointed.

Captain Zany, the park owner,

walked by.

When he heard about George's problem,

he smiled.

"Since monkeys don't grow very tall,

we have a special sign for them."

Was George tall enough now?

You bet he was!

HOW DOES IT MEASURE UP?

You will need:

Empty toilet paper roll

Empty paper towel roll

George's height changed depending on how he measured! Use your empty rolls to measure different things in your home. You could measure:

	Paper Towel Roll	Toilet Paper Roll
The length of your bed		
The height of the kitchen table		
The distance between the couch and the TV		

Do you get the same answer when you measure with the paper towel roll and the toilet paper roll? Which one gave you a bigger answer? Which one was smaller?

CHART YOUR HEIGHT

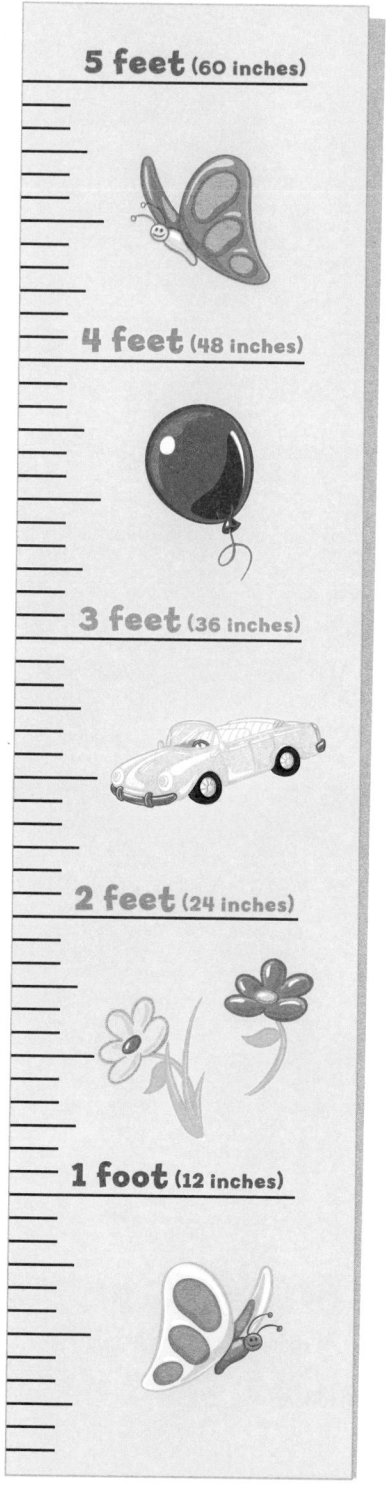

5 feet (60 inches)

4 feet (48 inches)

3 feet (36 inches)

2 feet (24 inches)

1 foot (12 inches)

You will need:

- A long sheet of paper or some paper grocery bags cut open and taped together

- A pencil

- A ruler

- Crayons, paints, markers, or stickers

Use your ruler and pencil to mark inches on one side of the paper.

Make sure your chart is at least 60 inches tall (that's 5 feet!).

Decorate the rest of your chart any way you like.

Tape your chart to the wall. Make sure the bottom touches the floor.

Stand with your back against the chart. Ask a partner or grown-up to mark your height on the chart.

Add the date each time you measure and watch yourself grow over time!

S0-CAP-063

WITHDRAWN